Marta Maretich

THE POSSIBILITY OF LIONS

Marta Maretich is a poet and fiction writer. Her work has appeared in *The Harvard Review*, *The Georgia Review* and *The Jacaranda Review*. Marta was editor of *The Berkeley Poetry Review* and *Whispering Campaign*, a journal of arts and literature. She has been awarded artist residencies at Yaddo and Norton Island, Maine. Marta Maretich lives in London.

First published by GemmaMedia in 2011.

GemmaMedia
230 Commercial Street
Boston, MA 02109 USA

www.gemmamedia.com

Printed in the United States of America

15 14 13 7 8

978-1-936846-02-3

Library of Congress Cataloging-in-Publication Data
Maretich, Marta.
The possibility of lions / Marta Maretich.
p. cm.
ISBN 978-1-936846-02-3 (pbk.)
1. Nigerians—California—Fiction. 2. Refugees—Fiction.
3. Families—Fiction. I. Title.
PS3613.A7398P67 2011
813'.6--dc23
2011022043

Cover by Night & Day Design

Inspired by the Irish series of books designed for adult literacy, Gemma Open Door Foundation provides fresh stories, new ideas, and essential resources for young people and adults as they embrace the power of reading and the written word.

Brian Bouldrey
North American Series Editor

GEMMA
Open Door

For Ruth and Frank, with love.

ONE

The suitcase was small, made of green and blue plaid canvas with a black plastic handle. A zipper made the circuit of one side like a golden racetrack. Mercy unzipped this, then she zipped it again, enjoying how smoothly the teeth locked together, how tightly they clenched to close the case. Then she unzipped the lid completely, flipped the soft top back and began to fill the suitcase with her most precious things.

She knew the problem with having too many treasures, or ones that were too big: you couldn't carry them. Mercy kept hers small and portable. She knew what mattered. A large box of crayons, the thin grown-up kind, with skin color included. A pad of paper. Her striped bathing suit, because if you were lucky you would get to swim where you were going. A stuffed rabbit. A liverwurst sandwich, nice and flat, in a thin plastic baggy. Her copy of *Yertle the Turtle* by Dr. Seuss. At the last moment she included a pair of pins, two sleek cats with rhinestone eyes, that her grandmother had given her for her last birthday. They were small, and they might be valuable. Mercy guessed you could trade them if you got into real trouble.

She closed the suitcase and slid the zipper around its track with satisfaction. It made a tight seal. She carefully folded, then rolled, one of Irene's dishtowels into a round pad the way Imelda had shown her, and she placed this on her head. Then she lifted the case and balanced it on the pad. After a moment she took her hands away and began, carefully, to walk.

She went down the long shadowy hall using smooth, ladylike steps. Her rubber flip-flops kissed her heels lightly as she went. She glided past the room her father was using as an office. A few steps farther took her past the door to her parents' room, closed and locked. She paused and listened but heard nothing. It was Saturday morning. From the family room came the sound of cartoons—screeches, bangs, the roar of canned laughter. Stephen would be up and watching in his pajamas, soupy brown Cocoa Puffs dissolving in a bowl, his eyes still swollen with sleep or crying. Mercy slipped through the living room to avoid him. She managed to pull open the heavy glass sliding door with one hand and descended the cement steps onto the patio, head held high, with only a slight wobble when she bumped the corner of the suitcase against the doorframe.

Outside, the sun had just come up over the tall redwood fence, but the day was already hot. She closed the door behind her, shutting in the cool, stale air. Out on the shady cement patio, she commenced pacing back and forth, queenly. The suitcase was comfortable on her head. It reassured Mercy that she could carry her things by herself now. She could carry it like this for miles, or as long as it would take to get away.

For a whole year after the McCalls arrived in the town, nobody except Bill's sister, Aunt Alice, knew that they were refugees. How would they know? The family looked like everyone else. They spoke English. Bill McCall worked in the oil fields like so many local men. Irene was a trained teacher, though she wasn't working. There was nothing special about the two kids, nothing that obviously set them apart, except for the little girl's stubborn habit of carrying everything on her head.

Their sudden arrival in town was nothing unusual. Just about every single person in Bakersfield came from somewhere else, and most had come recently. The town had been nothing more than a dusty farming center not long ago, standing all alone in the southern end of the San Joaquin Valley. Now, at the end of the sixties, Bakersfield was growing fast. People were attracted by the oil business and the profits to be made from the cotton, grain and fruit crops that stretched out in all directions around the town. In a boomtown, no one asks why you came there. No one was curious about the McCalls.

Mercy soon learned that even if she took the trouble of explaining how her family got to Bakersfield, people didn't understand. Children in her class, teachers, neighbors, ladies at the checkout in the supermarket: they looked at her with confusion when she tried to tell them how the war had come suddenly, how they had walked out the front door of their house in Port Harcourt with only one big brown Samsonite suitcase, how her father had stayed behind for three months, then come back to America without a job. The people she tried to tell didn't really know what Mercy was talking about, except the part about losing your job. They sympathized with that. But it seemed like not a single person in Bakersfield had ever heard of a place called Nigeria. Some people only had a foggy idea of where Africa was.

At the beginning, Mercy saw no reason to hide the past. She had been born in Nigeria, in Port Harcourt. This was something she was proud of; it made her special. Irene had told her the story of her birth many times. In the maternity ward of the Delta Clinic, Irene had braced her foot against the ribs of a birdlike midwife, Sister Bushwell, and out slid little Mercy, as slippery as a fish. Sister Bushwell had a job hanging on to her, Irene said, but she did it, laughing all the time and making Irene laugh, too. Being born in Nigeria had been fun.

Now, when Mercy said she came from Africa, people treated her like she was lying. Bakersfield people were the sort who prided themselves on being naturally smart. They might not be educated, but they were impossible to fool. And though they were prepared to humor a little girl up to a point, they had an unshakeable idea about the kind of person who came from Africa. Mercy's straight blond hair and pale skin told them all they needed to know about who she really was, where she really belonged.

The one exception was a skinny boy at school, a few years older. There was something slightly wrong with him—he wore an Army surplus jacket to school and his eyes were uneven, like the eyes of two different people. But they both lit up when he heard about Mercy. She took his reaction for interest. For days afterwards, though, he followed her around at recess hissing a single word over and over again in a voice just loud enough for Mercy and no one else to hear. Mercy recognized the word as the worst one white people used to talk about black people. The strange boy, trailing her to the swings in his dirty green jacket, tilting his head to keep her in his sights, seemed overjoyed to have the opportunity to use it, as though it had been burning a hole in his mind for a long time. There were no black children at their school. For him Mercy was the next best thing, because she came from Africa.

The teachers put a stop to the boy's hissing when they found out about it, but they couldn't hide their knowing smiles.

After that, Mercy kept quiet. Her brother Stephen never seemed to have these kinds of problems because he never said anything to anyone about Nigeria. He didn't talk about the past at all, not even with Mercy or Irene. Mercy thought this was because leaving their old life didn't matter as much to Stephen. Unlike her, he wasn't really African. Stephen had been born in an ordinary American hospital, in Carmel, California. Irene said his birth had been very difficult. A doctor had to finally pull him out with a pair of tongs, leaving a little dent in Stephen's head. No one caught him like a fish, no Nigerian nurse was there to laugh. That was his bad luck.

TWO

By the summer of 1968, the McCalls had been in Bakersfield for almost exactly one year. They were just beginning to get used to the way things were when, all at once, things changed again: their war came on the television.

It was June. School had just ended. Mercy and Stephen were spending the days swimming in the little rubber-lined pool in the back yard while their mother watched them from the shade of the patio. Now, still wearing their damp suits, they sat staring at the TV while they waited for Irene to fix them supper.

The news came on. Normally one of them would have changed the channel, but they were both too sleepy, drunk with sun. Before they knew it, half-familiar images were moving across the screen: wet mud roads, a tank turning a corner, soldiers in crumpled uniforms filing past the camera, glancing shyly up into the lens. The television set was black and white, but Mercy still remembered the colors: the roads were red, the bush was dark green. The soldiers' uniforms were a duller gray-green, the same color as their rifles. Sitting beside Stephen on the sofa, she put the fingers of her left hand in her mouth and began to suck them.

"Bill!" Irene was suddenly there, watching too, standing halfway to the kitchen holding a long wooden spoon in her hand. She had been mixing Kool-Aid in a pitcher and the spoon was stained bright orange. "Come see this!"

"Biafra," said the English commentator. Now the screen was showing pictures of streams of people, men in slack white shirts, women in long wrappers. They pushed bicycles loaded with bundles or carried laden basins on their heads. Mercy studied their faces carefully. The young soldiers had all been strangers, but these looked like people she might know. She searched the line of refugees for her nanny, Imelda, and Joseph, the gardener. She looked for Francis, the driver, in his pressed uniform with the insignia on the shoulder, and Okone the boy who ran errands for Irene.

"Where are they going?" Mercy

looked at Stephen. He didn't answer. He was watching Irene, not the screen.

"Bill!" Irene's voice cracked. "Come quick!" She dropped onto the sofa beside the children, still holding the dripping spoon.

"It's the war, kids. It's our—Oh!" she cried out as though in pain. A white nun, dressed all in white, held a naked boy before the camera. His arms and legs were as dark and thin as winter branches, silhouetted against the nun's pure white habit. His head was massive and his ribcage jutted out, reminding Mercy of the ribs of Sister Bushwell. The boy didn't look into the camera; he looked off to the side. Then, as if following his line of sight, the film cut to the background, a compound full of starved children, some lying curled on the ground, some standing and staring, bellies swollen like kettles.

Irene started to cry.

"We don't know them," Mercy said to herself. Now she was sure.

Bill McCall appeared in the doorway. He was wearing a yellow terrycloth bathrobe over his swimming trunks. In his hand he carried a long machete, a tool he used for gardening.

"Home sweet home," Bill said with an angry little laugh, glancing at the screen. "Didn't I tell you? Didn't I say this would happen? Hey?"

He turned and paced away down the hall. They could hear his bare feet hitting the floor. Suddenly he appeared in the doorway again.

"Are you ready to buy the tickets, Irene? Ready to get back on that plane?"

He whirled around and stalked off again. Irene leapt up and went after him. The children heard the door to the bedroom close, the button lock click shut. They heard their parents shouting.

"That's not home," Mercy said with certainty. Her words were muffled by her fingers.

"Shut up," said Stephen and slapped her, not very hard, on her sunburned arm.

THREE

Pictures of the Nigerian war started appearing every night on the television. More pictures of the starving children were printed in the newspapers and on the cover of *Life* magazine. There seemed to be no end to it, and no solution. People who had never showed any interest before started asking them questions about living in Nigeria. How did they manage to live in a place like that? Had their lives been in danger all the time? Had they starved, too? Mercy learned that the only thing worse than people not knowing anything about the place you came from was people knowing a little bit and the wrong things.

Even Aunt Alice was impressed by the images, and she was a hard lady to impress. She had lots of ideas she'd been keeping to herself since her brother's family had arrived in town. Now they all came out.

"I don't know how you could have lived in that place for so long. I mean, Billy always liked the life overseas, I never understood why, it must have been the pay, but with children? My Lord, those *people*. You see what they do to each other, what they're capable of." She shook her head with a laugh that sounded like Bill's.

The women were sitting at the secondhand dining room table Irene had recently bought at the Goodwill. It filled the area between the kitchen and the patio doors, a space that had been standing empty for a year because Irene hadn't wanted to buy any furniture, in case they moved back to Nigeria. In front of them, there were glasses of iced tea on new coasters, sweating with condensation. Despite the heat, Irene was wearing a high, curled wig of hair much darker than her own. Aunt Alice had gray hair, cut short like a man's. She said it was nice and cool like that.

"You must have been so relieved to get back here," she persisted. "Where it's safe, regular. I mean, you wouldn't ever go back *there*? Not *now*?"

"It's out of the question," Irene said in a dull voice. "Now."

"I'm very glad to hear you say that, Irene. You used to talk about going back when you first got here and I used to look at you and wonder what the *hell* you were thinking." Her tone was triumphant. She poked the ice in her glass with her finger. "You see how well it's all worked out."

Mercy, listening, waited for Irene to answer back. Was it really all worked out? Was this it? Someone needed to argue with Aunt Alice, to tell her that there were no pictures on television of the Nigeria they had lived in. But Irene didn't say anything; she took a sip of tea and hid her thoughts away under her wig.

FOUR

Mercy made a list in her head of good things that were true about Nigeria:

The summer thunder was so strong it shook the glass in the windows. Every afternoon, the rain clouds threw solid-looking rainbows right down to the horizon. Geckoes with dew-drop toes did pushups on the ceiling. Summer days tasted like orange slivers of papaya.

What else?

The market lady's favorite dress was made of yellow eyelet with a head wrapper to match, so excitingly high and crisp it looked like it might shatter if you touched it. She kept a huge glass jar of multicolored confetti on the counter. She sold this by the handful and when you put the tiny squares in your mouth they turned into chewing gum.

What else?

There were friends, families who lived in the other houses in the oil company compound, colleagues of Bill's. Men in short-sleeved white shirts and khaki pants who came over to smoke cigars and drink fat round glasses of brandy while their wives heated casseroles and the children played in the sprinklers. Where were they all now? The last time Mercy had seen any of them was on the plane that flew them out of Port Harcourt, sweaty, crumpled, frightened, each with a single suitcase in the hold. When the plane touched down, they scattered, who knew where.

Irene had made albums with photographs of some of the things and people Mercy remembered, but there hadn't been room for them in the big brown suitcase on the day they had to leave. Irene replaced the albums on the bookshelf in the front room. Then they carefully locked all the windows and doors and got in the Volkswagen and drove, passing roadblocks, tanks and what looked like a dead man in the ditch, to the airport. After they saw the body of the man, Irene made Mercy and Stephen crouch down in the footwell with their arms covering their heads. Mercy remembers the straight lines made by the raised ridges of the floor mats, the smell of rubber and dust.

For a long time, they believed they would come back and take the albums from the shelf and open them, restoring reality. But that summer when the pictures came on the television, Bill heard that the battle lines had passed back and forth through the walled compound where their house was five or six times. The houses there had no doors or windows now. Everything inside had been stolen. The soldiers had used the furniture and books as fuel for their cooking fires.

Irene locked herself in the bedroom for a whole day when she heard this. Mercy stood by the door, wondering if her mother had died, the way she sometimes said she wanted to. But Irene came out the next morning wearing the heavy dark wig and a pair of huge sunglasses covering her green eyes. She put Mercy and Stephen in the back seat of her Chevy Nova and got behind the wheel. As they backed out of the driveway, they saw Bill standing on the steps. He didn't try to stop them.

FIVE

Irene drove fast through the streets of Bakersfield. She took the new freeway, sliding down the onramp into empty lanes. They exited in the oldest part of town where wooden houses with wide porches sat in large plots of garden. Many of these had been turned into businesses—real estate offices, dental practices, beauty salons. Mercy and Stephen's pediatrician had his practice in one of them and for a minute Mercy wondered if Irene were taking them there. Stephen had a bad stomach and it seemed she was always sitting in the waiting room looking at picture books about Jesus while the doctor and Irene tried to figure out what was wrong with him.

But they passed the pediatrician's office with its signboard standing on the front lawn. They came to a street lined with tall trees and Irene pulled up at the curb in front of a small white house with a screened porch. A long banner tied across the porch railing said *Safariland U.S.A.*

Irene breathed a deep sigh as she set the parking brake. She looked at the children in the rearview mirror. The dark lenses of her sunglasses were like the eyes of a large insect. "How would you two like to see a lion?" she said. Her tone of voice was hopeless, as though she didn't believe the offer she was making.

Entering from the bright sunlight outside, at first they couldn't see anything in the darkness of the screened porch.

As their eyes adjusted they made out a black man seated behind a table at one end of the porch. "Welcome to Safariland," he said. When he smiled at them, they saw the white of his teeth, with a gap in the middle. His pale blue shirt floated like a cloud in the dim light. In an accent they had never heard before, he told them the entry fee for one adult and two children would be three dollars.

Mercy couldn't take her eyes off the man. She had only seen two or three black people since they had arrived in Bakersfield, and they had always been at a distance. These had been Americans, who looked different. This man, she knew without asking, was African.

"Don't stare like that," Irene hissed

to Mercy as she rummaged in her handbag for the money. "There's nothing to stare at."

"Look at what Stephen's doing," Mercy said, pointing. Stephen had moved to the other side of the table and was standing next to the man with the cashbox. He put his small hand on the man's arm as though to test that he was real.

"Yes?" The man tilted his head to one side and looked at him.

"What tribe are you from?" Stephen asked. He had been thinking the same thing Mercy had.

Irene let out a cry. "Stephen! It's very rude to ask people that in America." She began to apologize but the man laughed and waved his hand to show he wasn't offended. Then he drew himself up straight and looked at Stephen down his nose.

"What tribe do you think?" His head was round and his eyes were set deep in his skull. His skin was a medium brown. He was young, not thirty. Mercy noticed he had no tribal scars on his cheeks.

Stephen smiled bashfully. "I don't know. Efik?"

The man raised his eyebrows. "No, no, no. Not even close. Try again."

"Igbo?"

"Are you joking? With this fine profile?" He pretended to be scandalized.

"Are you—are you—Welsh?" The accountant who worked for Bill's department in Nigeria was Welsh. He, too, had a funny accent.

"Welsh! You can do better than that!"

he scoffed, trying hard not to laugh. Mercy saw him raise his eyebrows at Irene who had pushed her sunglasses up on her forehead and was smiling. Stephen looked uncertain.

"I am Bantu," the man offered when he saw Stephen couldn't think of what to say. He took Stephen's hand and shook it gently. "But your guesses were good."

"Bantu," Stephen repeated, memorizing the name of this tribe, which was new to him.

"You can call me Boniface." Boniface tore three red tickets off a large carnival roll and handed them to Stephen, chuckling. "Welsh! He's a good boy."

SIX

The back yard of the house was an ordinary one, with a wooden garage standing to one side and a low chain-link fence separating it from the property next door. Around a huge oak tree that grew at the far end of the yard, someone had built another enclosure of chain-link with panels eight feet high. Inside this, a male African lion slept in the shade of the tree.

Mercy threaded her fingers through the diamond-shaped openings of the fence and stared. The lion lay with its head stretched out, its white chin almost touching the trunk of the tree. The tip of its tail rested in a bright blue basin of water, twelve feet away. A strong smell of dust, raw meat and wild animal hung in the hot, still air. It was almost overpowering.

"It's a *lion*," Mercy breathed. It was strange to see a lion in a back yard that looked just like Aunt Alice's, who lived close by. Its presence seemed to open up infinite possibilities for finding lions in unexpected places.

"It certainly is," Irene said, taking her little Kodak camera out of her handbag. Stephen was working himself around to the other side of the cage, moving hand over hand along the fence, never taking his eyes off the animal.

"But he's not doing anything," Mercy said after a moment.

"He must be tired." Irene put the

lens into one of the gaps in the chain-link and took a picture.

"Why is he tired?"

Irene answered without thinking. "Because he's traveled a long way."

"But why?" Inexplicably, the presence of the sleeping lion was making Mercy feel a strange sense of longing. She didn't really want him to wake up. She wanted to lie down in the space between his huge paws and stay there, safe.

Irene put the camera down and looked straight at her so Mercy knew her mother meant business. "So we can see him, silly. They want to make a kind of zoo out by the river and keep him there so we can go visit him any time we want. With other animals like giraffes and hippos. Wouldn't that be nice?"

"Yes," Mercy watched the lion for another minute in silence. A fly crawled over his dark muzzle. "I think he's dead," she said.

"God forbid!" said a man's voice beside them. "Don't say that. Don't even think it!"

Mercy looked up to see a tall man with a dark beard. He had long hair combed back from his forehead, reaching down to the collar of his shirt. He was wearing a khaki bush jacket with many pockets. A yellow silk scarf was knotted around his neck. He came up to the cage and stood between her and Irene.

"A thing you need to know about the male lion," he said in a smooth, foreign voice, "is that he is extremely lazy.

Did you know about that? No? I bet you thought lions should be out hunting and killing, leaping. Biting, action-packed. Not so."

The bearded man turned toward Irene. "It will not surprise madame that it is only the lionesses who work hard. The male lions just lie there all day waiting for the ladies to bring them dinner."

"In fact, I did not know that," Irene said firmly. "But somehow it doesn't surprise me. You must be the owner."

"Anatole Hachette. So pleased to meet you." The man in the safari jacket held out his hand to Irene. Irene told him her name, all the time looking down at his hand holding hers. To Mercy, the man said, "Would you like me to wake up this lazy Roland?"

Mercy thought this was a bad idea, but she nodded because the tall man seemed to expect it. Her heart started to beat rapidly when she saw him go to the door on one end of the enclosure and open it with a large key. He stepped inside and closed the door after him but didn't lock it.

The lion lifted up its head and looked at him over its shoulder. It blinked its yellow eyes and made a grumbling noise deep in its throat. Then it hauled itself to its feet and plodded the few steps over to where the man was standing holding out his hand. The lion placed his great black nose in the man's hand, then licked his palm. His body was dun-colored, coated on one side with fine gray Bakersfield dust. His mane was full, golden at the roots and black at the tips as though badly dyed. The man thrust his fingers deep into the thick hair and started scratching. He looked up at them and smiled a dazzling smile. "You see," he said. "I am no more than Roland's human alarm clock. Without me he would sleep all day."

"Look at him!" Irene said with excitement. Her face was shining with happiness. She placed the camera up against the fence and took a picture.

The lion closed its eyes and leaned its weight into the man's thighs. It yawned, showing black lips and sharp yellow teeth. Mercy thought she could smell its meaty breath.

"Why don't you come in here," the man said to Irene.

Irene pulled the camera away from her face and stared at him. "Me?"

"Why not? Roland is a gentleman. He would never harm a lady." A little smile lingered on his face. It showed he didn't think Irene would say yes.

"Are you sure?" Irene said, moving unhesitatingly toward the cage door. She had her hand on the handle. Stephen was suddenly there, standing beside her. He grabbed the hem of her cotton blouse.

"It's all right," she said to him, pulling the fabric out of his hand. "Nothing's going to happen to me." Before he could say anything, she had handed him her purse and the camera and stepped through the cage door.

Hachette wasn't anticipating this. Her speed and confidence as she came into the cage surprised him—and the lion. The big cat swiveled his head around quickly and looked directly at her.

"Not so fast," Hachette warned. Irene stopped in her tracks, her face radiant. "Let him come to you."

Mercy watched her mother compose herself. Irene took a deep breath and stood still, not looking directly at the lion. She gave a little wave to Stephen, who watched her, pale, from the other side of the chain-link, and to Mercy who was doing all she could not to rattle the fence and start shouting. After what seemed like a year, the lion slid across the enclosure and approached Irene. He sniffed her bare, plump knee. She put out a hand and touched him.

SEVEN

The story came out during that first afternoon, the first of many they spent hanging on the wire of Roland's cage. Anatole Hachette, Boniface Bilebu and Roland came from the Congo. They had all been born there, but Anatole's family was from Belgium and so the government made him leave—Irene didn't press for details about exactly why. Boniface came along with Anatole Hachette for the adventure. Roland came too, because he belonged to Anatole Hachette and had no choice.

All this was very easy for the McCalls to believe. But what was Anatole Hachette doing in Bakersfield? Irene was half right when she said he was trying to establish a zoo. His idea was to take a thousand empty acres of land along the banks of the Kern River where it came down out of the mountains to the east of the town. The land here was too poor to farm; they only used it for grazing sheep now. His plan was to turn this waste ground into Safariland, a game park stocked with African animals. There would be herds of antelope and gazelle, giraffes and zebras, monkeys of all kinds, chimpanzees, leopards, cheetahs and, of course, lions, all wandering free. Visitors from all over the world would pay to drive Land Rovers through the park to see the animals at close range.

This was a new idea in 1968. Everyone in Bakersfield made their money from land in one way or another. Nobody had ever thought of using land this way before. It seemed a little crazy, but there was something about the way Anatole Hachette explained Safariland that made the notion of letting African animals loose in California seem reasonable. Anatole wasn't a young man—he must have been older than Bill—but he spoke of his plans with childlike enthusiasm. He painted a vivid picture of the new life his park would bring to an empty stretch of scrubland and the people who heard him caught the spirit of possibility. This, Mercy thought much later, must have been what drew Irene to him. It wasn't because she was in love with him, as Bill feared. It was because he was not afraid of ending up in Bakersfield. Just the opposite: he chose to be there because he believed it could be transformed into something better. To make this happen, he was ready to put everything he had on the line: he was bringing his own lions.

After that first meeting, Irene threw herself behind Anatole Hachette's project. Safariland had already collected a few volunteers, people drawn in by Anatole's vision. But Irene was a good typist and well organized, with a flair for alphabetizing. All through that summer she worked for Safariland without pay. She wrote letters to important people for Anatole, whose written English was nothing to brag about. She made appointments for him and kept Safariland's accounts. Sometimes she even bought bags of groceries for Anatole and Boniface

Bilebu, a thing she warned the children not to mention to Bill.

Almost immediately, this activity seemed to cheer Irene up. She put her dark wig away on a white head-shaped stand in her bedroom. Instead she wore silk scarves over her pale brown hair, saying it was less fussy for the summer. Her sunglasses stayed in her handbag with her Lucky Strike cigarettes. Her beautiful green eyes shone with purpose.

When the news came on now with pictures from Nigeria, Stephen and Mercy raced to the television as fast as they could and fought one another to be the one to turn it off.

EIGHT

Bill McCall now had a job managing an oil lease on the west side of the valley. It was a small outfit that ran out of a single trailer. One day when she had things to do in the Safariland office, Irene suggested that he take Mercy and Stephen out to see where he worked.

It was a long drive in the cab of Bill's white pickup, the two children buckled into a single seatbelt on the hard seat because Irene insisted. They set off early in the morning. Bill had on his yellow hardhat and his black Red Wing shoes and the children wore shorts and identical blue flip-flops, one size apart. By the time they reached the city limits, the sun coming through the windshield was burning their bare thighs. The truck had no air conditioning or radio because it was a company truck. Bill drove with one hand on the wheel, one arm hanging out the open window. He worked a toothpick from one side of his mouth to the other, thinking his own thoughts.

The trailer was parked in the middle of the oil fields, in a yard fenced with chain-link. It had a couple of big gray desks in it, some green filing cabinets and a pair of shiny black telephones. No one else worked there but Bill. The only window looked out on a view of a pumpjack rocking up and down against a background of white sky. Beyond, there were more of them scattered across the dry, sandy hills. From a distance they looked like horses bucking in slow motion. Close up, they looked like what they were: pumps. You could hear the hum and click of the mechanism, the buzz of the cables moving over the winch.

"Are they drilling for oil?" Stephen asked.

"Dirty water," Bill said. "The wells you can see are all tapped out."

Bill didn't seem to know what to do with Mercy and Stephen once they were there. He made a call while the children sat on the empty desk, kicking their heels against the aluminum sides until they produced a sound like thunder. For a while, Bill took no notice: he was half deaf, Irene said, from being shelled on Guadalcanal. Finally he heard the noise they were making and shouted at them to keep quiet. When he got off the phone he said they had to drive to another part of the lease, where his workers were drilling.

A swamp cooler kept the inside of the trailer tolerable, but the minute they stepped outside, the heat pressed in around their bodies. It pounded down from the sky, bounced off the aluminum sides of the trailer and radiated back up from the packed earth of the yard. They could feel it through the thin rubber soles of their flip-flips and on the backs of their calves. Mercy put her hand on the top of her head. Her hair felt like a smooth, hot skillet. She turned around and went back to the steps of the trailer.

Bill let her stay behind. She watched him and Stephen drive out of the yard and down the dirt road to the main road. She watched until the white truck disappeared into the heat haze, feeling slightly scared to be left alone. All she wanted was to go home and swim in the pool. Or maybe go over to Safariland and sit beside Irene as she filed.

Back in the trailer, she played with the water cooler, the only exciting thing there. It belched silver bubbles into its glass bottle when you opened the spigot, and dispensed fascinating pleated paper cups. She pulled them out one by one. She teased out their folds to make fat barrel shapes that she stacked on the top of the desk.

Bill returned. The heat had made

Stephen sick, and so he called Irene to come and get them. They had to wait a long time for her to get there. While they waited, Bill made Mercy straighten every single paper cup and replace it as best she could in the dispenser.

NINE

Bill laughed out loud the first time he saw a picture of Anatole Hachette in the newspaper.

"Is this your guy?" he said to Irene, flapping the paper at her. It showed a picture of Anatole wrestling with Roland. The lion stood on his back legs with his paws on Anatole's shoulders, his mouth open. It looked like the two of them were dancing. "Your great white hunter?"

"He's not a hunter," Irene said. She was folding towels and she went on folding them, first in half, then in quarters then, in her own special flourish, in thirds. "He's starting a wild animal park. I told you."

"I don't know about that," Bill said. Up until now he hadn't shown much interest in Safariland. "He took those rich Italian farmers hunting, didn't he? What's their name? It sounds like they wiped out every living thing in the place. No wonder they booted him out."

"Bill, you probably know better than anyone why he had to leave the Congo," Irene said. "It was just like us."

"It was not just like us," Bill said seriously. "Nigeria is a different story."

"Well," Irene said, folding decisively, "I'm not sure I really know how it was for us, let alone him. But if by the Italian couple you mean the Ambrosinis, then, yes, it's true: he did take them on safari a few years ago. That's how they know him. That's why they invited him here and that's why they're donating their land to the park."

"So that's how he got his foot in the door," Bill mused. He'd never come to Safariland headquarters to meet Anatole Hachette in person, though Irene had invited him. He said he'd meet him when he needed to. Irene said he was jealous. She said Bill wanted life to be as little fun as possible because it suited his view of the world.

Bill read over the article. "This is insanity," he said. "They have lions here already."

Irene stopped folding and looked at her husband fiercely. "Oh, please," she said.

"But they do." He chuckled to himself.

"You're telling me there are lions here? In Bakersfield? What kind of lions?"

"Californian lions, of course."

"There are no such things!"

"They call them mountain lions, or pumas, in Spanish. They live right up in the mountains. You don't believe me? Ask our local expert, our very own Indian."

"You don't mean old Bernardo," Irene put her hands on her hips. Bernardo was a relation of Aunt Alice's husband, Uncle Paul. He was an ancient, barrel-chested man with dark skin who lived in a cabin about an hour's drive into the mountains. Aunt Alice said he was 100 years old, and that seemed possible. He looked like a Mexican, but Bill always insisted he was an Indian.

"Sure. He told me all about it. Mountain lions, bears, wolves, antelope. Sure. Eagles."

"I've never heard anything like that, Bill. Not from anyone."

"I guess you haven't been talking to the right people." Bill tried to return to reading the newspaper, but Irene persisted.

"So if they have all those animals here," she said, "why don't we ever see them? The only thing I've ever seen here is a sheep. And one coyote, once."

"They're up in the mountains," Bill insisted, his eyes a little shifty. "Talk to Bernardo. You have to get right up there."

"I take it you've seen them yourself?"

Bill didn't answer. He tried to change the subject by holding up the newspaper photo in delight. "Look at that bush jacket, not a mark on it. I bet he gets it dry-cleaned. Do you think if I wore a jacket like that the city fathers would throw money at me, too?"

Irene walked out of the room, leaving the towels where they were. Out of the corner of his eye Bill watched her. He watched her every move.

TEN

Despite what Bill thought, things were going well for Anatole Hachette. As the summer wore on, the town's boredom increased and interest in Safariland grew. Anatole labored in the heat, building relations with local leaders, with realtors and landowners, car salesmen and members of the Chamber of Commerce. Dark stains spread in the armpits of his bush jacket. He gave lectures at stifling Rotary Club lunches and meetings of the Board of Supervisors. He performed publicity stunts, wrestling with Roland on the melting tarmac of car lots and malls. There was a steady stream of visitors to Safariland headquarters and pictures in the paper every week. Suddenly, everyone was asking why, of all the valley towns, only Bakersfield had no zoo. Safariland U.S.A. began to seem like something the town couldn't live without.

Mercy got sick of it. Safariland kept Irene busy and this meant hours spent waiting at the headquarters where there was no swimming pool and nothing much to do. Stephen didn't mind so much. He liked shadowing Boniface Bilebu, helping him when he worked on the engine of the Safariland truck. But Mercy just hung around pestering Irene until her mother lost her temper. Then she went outside and hung on Roland's cage.

The lion was just as lazy as Anatole Hachette said he was. Mercy was disillusioned with him; when Anatole wasn't there it was like someone had turned Roland's switch to OFF. She wondered what he'd do when he was free and living beside the rough waters of the Kern River with other, lady, lions. Would he have more energy? Would he get up off his backside and do something? She sidled up next to where he lay snoring and poked a stick through the mesh, touching his flank. His skin quivered, but he didn't wake up. She thought of going inside the cage, the way her mother had, but she knew she would get in deep, deep trouble with Irene for that. She doubted Roland would go to the trouble of eating her.

ELEVEN

The summer wore on. To keep the momentum up, Anatole decided to throw a party. It was really the Ambrosinis' idea. The couple, Ruby and Benito, were very flashy. They had a bronze Cadillac convertible which they drove to Los Angeles whenever they felt like it. They traveled in Europe and owned a boat and went on safari with Anatole Hachette. Irene, who had been there, said their ranch house was decorated all over with the animals they had shot themselves while they were in Africa with Anatole.

"It's fancy," she reported, "but it's not to my taste." Mercy got the impression she didn't exactly approve of the

Ambrosinis. But they were strong supporters of Safariland.

When Bill heard about the party, he said only people like the Ambrosinis would think that spending money was the way to make money.

Boniface Bilebu painted the living room yellow and stapled dried palm leaves to the ceiling so it would look like the inside of a hut. He installed narrow shelves around the walls and on them Irene and some other volunteers arranged Anatole Hachette's collection of Congolese masks, baskets, jewelry and statues. Mercy and Stephen had the job of filling a canoe with plastic flowers before it was suspended from the beams of the porch roof. On a card table in the middle of the room they set a papier-mâché model of Safariland: a thatched visitor's center and amphitheater, and animal enclosures stretching away along the banks of the Kern River. The man who made the model left out the animals, so Stephen set some of his plastic toys here and there, towering above the buildings.

Outside in the yard, between the house and Roland's enclosure, Anatole set up a rented dance floor. He bounded it with strings of lights and installed a makeshift bar at one end and a raised stage on the other. Boniface whistled through the gap in his teeth when he saw the arrangement.

"*Not bad, not bad. It looks like my favorite nightclub in Kinshasa,*" he said in French. "*Maybe this is a better way to make our money.*"

Mercy, standing nearby, listened to the musical sound of Boniface speaking French. His words in this language came easily, fast.

"*Don't speak too soon, BiBi,*" Anatole said, also in French, coming down off a ladder. "*Wait until you hear the band.*"

Boniface widened his eyes with horror. "*It isn't* country and western? *Please say no.*"

Mercy made out the words *country and western*, square boats sliding down a smooth river.

Anatole shook his head sadly and put a consoling hand on Boniface's shoulder. "*They call themselves* The Silver Bullets.

The head of the Chamber of Commerce *recommended them.*"

"*No!*"

"*We have to go with the local culture, Bibi. When in Rome etcetera.*"

Boniface groaned. "*In Rome, I promise you, you would be able to find some music you could dance to. Of all the strange places we have ended up, Hachette, this must be one of the strangest.*"

"*You don't have to tell me.*" Anatole sighed. He saw Mercy standing there and gave her a smile.

Boniface Bilebu looked at the stage and its proximity to the lion's cage. "*At least Roland will have the pleasure of biting* The Silver Bullets *on the ass,*" he said.

What silver bullets? Mercy thought. Where will they get bullets like that?

"*Maybe it would be better to put the bar over there?*" Anatole mused.

"*Maybe it would.*"

Mercy watched while the two men swapped the bar and the bandstand. Then they were ready to go.

TWELVE

On the night of the party, Irene curled her light brown hair using hard plastic curlers. She penciled in her fine eyebrows and put on lipstick the color of a pink shell. She let Mercy stay with her while she got dressed. She helped her mother choose a plain cream-colored dress with short sleeves and some Italian sandals that had a strap between the toes. Around her neck she fastened a string of amber beads the color of honey.

When they were ready to go, Bill came out wearing a red fez. Irene, disgusted, refused to go out the door until he took it off.

Some guests were already there when they arrived. The Ambrosinis were standing on the dance floor talking to Anatole. Ruby Ambrosini wore a multicolored minidress, like a lady in a magazine, and her long blond hair was teased up and combed back from her face into a kind of mane. Benito, much older, had on a bush jacket that looked like Anatole's, but brand new. The three of them were drinking champagne and they offered some to Bill and Irene. Bill drank his with his little finger cocked up and studied Anatole Hachette warily. At the sight of Anatole's silk neck scarf, sky blue on that night, he muttered to himself, "How come she lets him wear a costume?"

That night, Anatole Hachette was at his best. His dark, bushy head was haloed by strings of lights. He radiated warmth and generosity; men and women alike were drawn to him, the nucleus of the party. Flattery, jokes, stories of adventure flowed from him. He loved his own party and that made him even more attractive. He had been so bored in Bakersfield. Without saying as much, he knew they had all been bored, too. They needed him and he was delighted to bring them some relief. That night, Bakersfield embraced Anatole Hachette like a savior.

On the bandstand, The Silver Bullets began to play, quietly at first, the notes of the steel guitar bending on the warm night air. Boniface switched on the necklace of lights and the yard became a kind of theater. The guests began arriving. The mayor and his wife came early and drank champagne. The city councilors and their wives came after and were happy with wine or beer. The editor of the newspaper mainly wanted to eat and headed straight for the buffet table, loaded down with casseroles and salads and quivering constructions of Jell-O. Then came the vice president of the biggest oil company, a pair of newscasters, four or five rich farmers, the man who owned two restaurants and the head of the Rotary Club. And their wives. They kept coming: everyone Anatole invited showed up that night.

The men had short brushy haircuts, thin ties and tight, dark suits. The women had their hair in tall, fluffy hairdos. They wore sheath dresses and pale shoes with high heels and pointy toes. They carried clutch purses and never put them down all night, even much later, when the serious dancing began.

There were a few other children there, and Mercy and Stephen led them on an expedition to the deep dark end of the yard, where Roland's enclosure stood, forgotten. The children lined up along the side and peered in. They could smell the lion and feel the warmth coming off him, but all they could see in the dark was a shadowy mass. Mercy guessed Roland was asleep despite the noise. Stephen pretended he had the power to call him, like a dog, and make him come. When that had no effect the other children peeled off one by one and went running back to the lights of the party.

Irene found them and made them line up at the buffet table. Mercy and Stephen loaded their paper plates and went to sit with her on the grass to eat. She looked happier than she had in months. She smoked a cigarette, a smile playing at the corners of her mouth.

"This is going well," she said. "Maybe we're finally getting somewhere."

The party was in full swing now and the crowd was growing noisy. The band turned up the volume and two or three couples pushed near the bandstand, attempting to dance. Boniface Bilebu was at his station behind the bar, serving drinks. Bill was there, too, talking to Boniface. They watched Boniface throw back his head and laugh raucously at something Bill said.

"At least your father has found a friend," Irene said wryly, watching him.

The night went on. Mercy found herself under the buffet table, peeking out from beneath the tablecloth, watching people's feet as they milled back and forth. Someone dropped a glass of red wine and it splashed a woman's white shoes. A man in black dress shoes executed a shuffle-ball-change. Snakeskin cowboy boots ground out a cigarette butt and moved on. The last thing Mercy remembered was Anatole Hachette getting up on the bandstand.

"My honored beasts," she heard him say. The crowd lowed and barked and howled and whooped. From the other end of the yard, she thought she heard a loud roar but she was too sleepy to be sure. She curled up on the floor with her head resting on her palm and pretended she was lying safely in the space between Roland's paws.

Someone who smelled like Irene lifted Mercy up and carried her through the party. The music was playing very fast and very loud and people were shouting.

"What's that man doing?" Mercy caught a glimpse of the mayor standing on the bandstand beating one of Anatole's huge drums. His thin tie was thrown back over his shoulder and his face was shining with sweat. Dancers leapt and jiggled and waved their handbags crazily in the air.

"Put your head down, sweet thing," Irene said, slurring the words a little bit. She carried Mercy through the house and out to the car. Stephen was there, curled on the back seat.

THIRTEEN

In the morning she woke up in her own bed, staring at the underside of Stephen's bunk. The house was quiet and sun streamed in through the windows. She lay there listening to Stephen breathing through his mouth. She got up and went down the hall to the kitchen where she found Irene making French toast in her nightgown. Mercy had the feeling, for the first time in a long time, that everything was going to be fine.

In less than an hour, they knew the lion was loose. Someone had taken wire cutters to Roland's cage in the early hours of the morning and opened up a hole big enough for him to escape. For once, Roland had found the energy to get up. Anatole Hachette was out with the sheriff trying to find him before someone else did.

"I just know they're going to shoot him," Irene moaned.

"That would be against the law," Stephen said, without explaining why he thought so.

They watched the coverage on the local news.

"It's not a good thing," one local woman said when they asked what she thought about the lion being loose in town. "I don't keep pets myself."

"I was washing the car," one eyewitness said. "When I looked up and saw it. I called my wife and said, 'Look at this!' And she came out. And there it was. A great big," he gestured with his hands, "tiger."

By noon they had tracked Roland to a warehouse downtown, and a crowd was gathering. Some people brought their own guns, hopeful they'd have a chance to use them. There were rumors that the lion had attacked someone's dog, eaten a child. Fortunately, a man from the SPCA showed up in time and let Anatole Hachette shoot Roland himself with a tranquilizer dart.

Mercy watched it on film: Roland crouching behind some boxes, Anatole taking aim. Roland being hit by the dart and falling down. They showed the same pictures on the LA news later that night and on the national news the next day. It was like someone you know well becoming famous, but not in the right way.

"It was kind of too bad," said someone in the crowd. "But I'm glad they got him. I guess."

Irene was at Safariland headquarters that evening when the police came to deliver the court order. It gave Anatole Hachette just 24 hours to vacate.

Anatole Hachette did his best. He called the mayor, who made sympathetic sounds but couldn't do anything. He called the head of the Chamber of Commerce, who wouldn't come to the phone; his wife said he still had a hangover from Anatole's party. He tried number after number, running his hand through his disheveled hair. Everyone he spoke to gave him more bad news. Donations dematerialized, support disappeared, old debts were remembered. Other laws loomed up to block him. All the goodwill he had felt the night before vaporized in the afternoon sun.

Hunched over the receiver, Anatole looked exhausted and shrunken, a different man from the genial host of the night before. He was astounded by what was happening. "My lion hasn't harmed anyone," he argued, near tears. "The person who cut open the cage is the one who should be punished. Is anyone even looking for him?"

Meanwhile, Boniface Bilebu warmed up the truck.

FOURTEEN

When they finally got Roland out of the pound, Anatole and Boniface moved him to the only place they could, a shack the Ambrosinis lent him in the fields beyond the city limits. It stood on a plot of dusty ground by the side of a straight two-lane road, surrounded by fields that also belonged to the Ambrosinis. There was a big eucalyptus tree in front. Out back, row after row of grapevines stretched away toward the foothills.

When Irene took Mercy and Stephen out there a few days later, every vine had a little carpet of brown paper lying at its base and the red raisin grapes were laid out on these to dry. The air smelled of sugary juice and insecticide. There were wasps flying everywhere.

When they drove up, Boniface Bilebu stepped out of the house carrying a shotgun. He smiled when he saw them and tried to hide the gun behind his body. Irene didn't say anything about it out of politeness. To draw attention to the gun would mean pointing out how bad things had become. Irene had taken to wearing her dark wig again, and Boniface, likewise, didn't acknowledge any change in her.

"Hachette isn't here," he told them. He looked very tired. His skin was the color of ash. "He's in San Diego."

"You're all on your own?" Irene said, looking around. A pickup truck went by on the road, its radio blaring. Boniface stared after it suspiciously.

"I have quite a lot of company," he said grimly. "Everybody seems to know where to find us. They've cut the cage two times more this week."

"Doesn't the sheriff do anything?"

"He does not, madame." Boniface laughed. His eyes flickered down toward the shotgun. Then, catching the look on Stephen and Mercy's faces, he said. "But Roland is all right! He's fine. Do you want to see him?"

He led them around the side of the house to a lean-to made of sheet metal and draped with dirty tarpaulins.

"I do this to make it harder to find. But it doesn't help. I think they can smell him." Boniface pulled away a piece of aluminum siding to reveal a cage made of chicken wire. Inside, golden eyes staring out at them, was Roland.

They had never seen him so awake. He rose to his feet immediately and came to the wire, his yellow eyes alive and curious. He leaned against the flimsy chicken wire and it bulged with his weight. His mane stuck out through the mesh as though it were a hairnet. The children poked their fingers through and scratched his dusty skin.

"He's glad to see us," Mercy said, pleased.

"He wants you to take him away," Boniface said, running his hand over his face. There was an old couch pushed up next to the side of the cage and Mercy knew that this was where Boniface had been sleeping. Irene asked what Anatole was doing in San Diego.

"He's meeting a man at the zoo," Boniface said.

"The zoo?" Irene sounded alarmed. "I thought Anatole was trying to find some land on the coast?"

Boniface shook his head. "He owes so much money now. Rents, fines, meat bills, taxes. He has debts he didn't know he had. It's too much."

"Too much," Irene echoed in a breathy voice. She reached up and touched one of the curls of her wig. Mercy now saw it for what it was, a protective covering, like Bill's yellow hardhat. "But he'll be back soon. He's not going to leave you out here for long?"

Boniface shrugged. “He said he’d be back Sunday. Maybe Monday.” It was Friday afternoon and the whole week-end lay ahead.

“At least Roland is with you,” Mercy said, knowing that didn’t make things any better, knowing that was the problem.

Boniface Bilebu stood in the yard and watched them drive away. The children waved at him until the road dipped and they lost sight of him. When they turned around, they could see that Irene was crying silently. Driving steadily, even calmly, and crying. Stephen reached one arm through the gap between the seats and wiped her cheek with his sleeve.

That evening when Bill came home, Irene met him at the door. They stood talking for a minute in the entry hall, then Bill turned around and went out again. He didn't come home that night. Irene told the children he had gone out to stay with Boniface Bilebu until Anatole came back. He stayed away all the next day. Irene left the children with Aunt Alice and drove out to take him some clean clothes.

"But what is Daddy doing there?" Mercy asked when she got back. It was difficult to imagine Bill babysitting a lion. Or anything else.

Irene made light of it. "He and Boniface are playing cards, mostly."

On Sunday afternoon, Bill came home. "That's the end of it," he said. Anatole had returned. Bill helped him and Boniface load the lion into the truck. They were taking him to the zoo in San Diego.

"He had his tail between his legs," Bill said. Mercy thought he meant Roland.

"I suppose it's for the best." Irene tried to put a brave face on it. "They say it's a very good zoo."

"We can go visit him," Stephen suggested.

"Do you think Roland would be glad to see us?" Irene said, running her hand over his short hair.

"We won't ever go," Mercy said, fingers stuffed in her mouth. And they never did.

FIFTEEN

When September came, school started again. Nigeria was still on the evening news, but Mercy had a nice teacher that year. Miss Stevens had long brown hair and wore Bal à Versailles perfume so it was a pleasure just to stand next to her. She thought Mercy was smart and she thought the ability to carry things on your head was a definite talent, something not everyone was able to do.

Encouraged, Mercy practiced. She packed her suitcase a little fuller every time, adding a brown-haired Barbie, a china plate with the Lord's Prayer painted on it in spidery writing. When all this wasn't heavy enough, she added grown-up books from her parents' bookshelf until the weight of the case pressed hard on her skull bones and she struggled to hold her neck straight. She wobbled through the house like this until she had a headache. But there was no doubt about it now. Mercy needed to be ready to carry as much as she could, because the road might turn out to be very long and, after all, a person might never make it home again.